I0831508

JUSTICE

Scott Hughes

ISBN: 0-692-63699-4
ISBN-13: 978-0-692-63699-2

Library of Congress Control Number: 2016932852

Manchester, CT 06040

Published by OnlineBookClub.org

Dedication

I dedicate this and everything to my two children, Tristen and Amaya. I love you both. I hope to make you proud. All I want is to work to become as close as I can to the role model you deserve.

Contents

Preface

Sympathy shines the only light in the dark impassable tunnels constructed between all of us. Forever alone, destined for the abyss of existential annihilation, the dim light of sympathy provides not a rescue but a much needed comfort.

In our greatest tragedy, we frequently cast away that one light, lashing out at the dark instead, lashing out at anything and everything that surrounds us, in pain and fear with anger and hate.

The darkness within us all too often overcomes the dim light between us.

Part One

Bedroom

In the dimly lit bedroom, the young beauty stands, her thigh resting ever so lightly on the bed frame. She glances at the photo, its black encasement carefully matching the darkness of the painted wooden bed frame. She considers rotating the frame away or turning it face-down on the end table next to the flickering scented candle. That is what someone feeling guilty would do, right? But she doesn't feel guilty.

Brynn doesn't feel guilty when it comes to her husband anymore. When Brian arrives, she will have sex with him.

Brian isn't her husband, though.

She did not feel guilty the first time she had sex with Brian, not because she lacked the integrity needed to feel guilty the first time she cheated on her husband, but because Brian was not the first time.

She recalls meeting Brian. He introduced himself with some stupid joke about the similarity of their names. The joke was so lacking in funniness, she chose not to waste valuable brain neurons remembering it. In fact, she had recently read a *Daily Times* article containing this relatively useless fact: the typical human brain has one hundred billion neurons. The dumb joke was not even worth a single one of those one hundred billion neurons.

Many women love to say that they find a sense of humor the most attractive quality in a man. But she didn't zone out in Mrs. Hill's 10th Grade math class dreaming about bedding Chris Farley with his hundreds of pounds of hilariousness. Now Jeff Buckley, on the other hand, may have brought her GPA down a bit. Both men died, of course, but only the death of the latter broke her precious, childish heart.

Not as much as her crappy husband broke her heart, though. Her crappy husband, Marcus. *The asshole, Marcus.*

Does her infidelity make her awful?

Does it make her ten times as awful because she no longer feels bad about her infidelity?

No.

Oh, so she *used to* feel bad about doing something she shouldn't have been doing, right? But now in some kind of rationalizing habituation she *no longer* feels bad, right?

She *no longer* feels bad about doing something she *should* feel bad about, right?

Hell no!

The reality: back then, she did feel bad. She felt bad about something she should not have felt bad about.

Since then, she *learned.* Since then, she became more informed. It happens with time. She grew up. And now big-girl-Brynn sleeps with whoever she wants.

Well, she *sleeps* with her husband. But in the bed they share, she has *sex* with whoever she wants.

She does this whoever-she-wants-sexing while Marcus hangs out with his true love: his trivial job. Or she gets off *wherever* she wants while he lounges around the house in his dirty, worn pajamas like some neglected, overgrown child. Sometimes she wishes she could call the Department of Children and Families and have Marcus taken away and thrown in some kind of orphanage or foster home *or whatever.*

Well, it all used to upset her; the key phrase being *used to.* It *used to* make her miserable. It *used to* make her lonely.

Lonely misery kind of makes a girl angry, though.

Marcus never seemed to notice her constant misery, just her bursts of anger. *"Why do you always pick a fight with me over nothing?!"* Fucking Marcus. Fucking crybaby, '*poor me*' Marcus.

After a while, he started to sound like a broken record. Oh, he would change the words, but he would still say the same stupid crap.

All it ever meant was, *"I see you are mad, so now I will tell you I am madder about something else. In fact, I'm too mad to explain, so I will give you the silent treatment."*

You know, in movies and sensationalist media coverage, they always make it seem like the epitome of a crappy husband is a hitter. Of course, they call it *abuse*. But they only mean hitting, not abuse.

She even *used to* wish he would hit her. Then he would feel sorry for once. Then other people would feel sorry for her. Or maybe she would not tell. She would have leverage over him. He would appreciate her for doing him the favor. *"Thank you for not telling. Thank you for staying with me."*

She tried to tell people how he abused her. How he emotionally abused her.

Of course, she couldn't use the word abuse. If you say abuse, they assume you mean hitting. When they find out you don't mean hitting, they declare you Mrs. Melodramatic Liar, the nagging wife who fails to appreciate the horrors of real abuse. You can qualify the word abuse with the word emotional; you can say, "I'm being *emotionally* abused." Then they act like the word e-m-o-tional is spelled f-i-c-tional. They think you're *pedantically* melodramatic. People hate most adverbs. They want small talk, not to play mad libs or listen to you whine about your life.

Why would they believe her anyway? *'Marcus seems so nice,'* they would think. *'I have never even seen him raise his voice,'* they would think.

How do they expect a passive-aggressive jerk to act? Like a violent maniac?

She should have thrown herself down the stairs just so she could lie and say Marcus did it.

It would practically be true. He deserved it.

People love an abused wife story. They would eat it up. He would be guilty before 911 even arrived.

But she didn't do that. Marcus never hit her. Not yet, at least.

So instead, she let some guy at the gym show her the fifty states. Gregory. Gregory was no super catch. Gregory didn't rock her off her feet with his world-renowned charm and gym-toned body of steel. However, at least, he tried to impress her. He tried, which meant something. Sure, he did not try like an athlete tries in an Olympic race. But he wore clothes without holes in them when he would see her. He talked to her. He showed some real interest in her. So what if he hit on several other women at the gym. She still liked the polite attention.

She felt guilty that first time. She eased into it from there. First came a subtle make-out session in the gym parking lot. After that, they actually had a date—well, coffee followed by two rounds of drinks and two rounds of sex.

The funny thing about guilt is how close it lives to anger. It's like you feel both at the same time. What do people say? Two sides of the same coin?

She doesn't feel guilty anymore, but she doesn't feel so miserable and angry either.

She didn't get off the first time she had sex with Gregory that night. Why do we count how many times we have sex by how many times the guy gets off? The feminists need to look into that.

But both times with Gregory, it wasn't all about the sex. With Gregory, she enjoyed the anger of it, like jumping in a pool of sexual rage and breathing fire.

With the second man, Edward, she jumped instead into an ocean of sexual ecstasy.

The second man was anything but a second man. He brought her to a hotel room where he screwed her like a rag doll all night. It was dirty. It was sexy. It was rough. It was thrilling!

The second man gave her what Marcus could never have given her sexually: the luxury denied to any faithful wife.

Even if she had outright asked Marcus to be a little more spontaneous, a little more rough... *a little more freaky*, it never would have worked right. The excitement of rough, naughty sex is that it is thrilling, almost scary. Not in a horrific way, but just enough to keep your focus on the deed rather than straying to the dishes or the laundry *or whatever*. You cannot walk a man through it.

It's just the unspoken vows in marriage. You give up excitement for consistency. Give up freedom for loyalty. Give up fun for support. The typical married woman resigns herself to a life of sexual mediocrity.

You know this going in, unless you do something completely unpredictable, like get get married in some drunken tryst in Las Vegas to some hunk you just met that night.

So why go in at all?

It's worth it, of course.

Nobody wants to merely have great sex 24/7. Some people say they do, but they don't. The people who think about sex the most are probably just the people who get it the least.

Love is worth it.

Love is not merely consistency, loyalty, and support. Love is so much more. Love is something worth sacrificing for. Love is worth graduating from free party-girl to faithful partner. Love is worth growing from joyous child to dedicated housewife.

If you're lucky enough to have children—the gift of that purpose—love is worth abandoning your own dreams to share with your partner in helping your children achieve their dreams.

Love is worth it.

But what about when your partner reneges on his side of the trade? What about when instead of loyal, supportive love, you get taken for granted? Get treated like you're replaceable? Like everything you do is wrong no matter how hard you try?

What do you do when you sacrifice everything for nothing?

What do you do then?

Do you stay loyal to someone who deserves the opposite? Do you keep old promises to someone who should have never received that honor in the first place?

No, you seek out the happiness you deserve. And, if that happiness is not attainable because it was stolen by the real vow-breaker, well then you get whatever pleasure you can.

She will take that well-deserved pleasure shortly when Brian arrives. She will take it right where Marcus sleeps at night. It's what she deserves. It's fair. It's justice.

Part Two

Traffic

On a crowded highway at 5:30pm on a warm Tuesday in autumn, the 30-year-old man sits in a black Nissan Altima. His black Nissan Altima. He rubs a hand through his short black hair, his tie already loosened, the perfect daily cliché of his mid-level employment at a software company. Glare from the sun fights its way through ever-changing paths—bouncing off vehicles, smearing on windshields, sneaking between the cracks of visors. He sighs after yet another abrupt press on the brake. A man can handle driving slowly, but the stop and go of rush hour truly tests a man's patience.

Marcus can handle it, though. Marcus has a reputation for his incredible patience.

Others might even say he never gets angry. To say he never gets angry seems not quite accurate. They do not see Marcus yell or scream or punch anyone. Indeed, he does not do such things. When people act that way, it's not just that they are angry. That is why, when those kinds of people who do those kinds of things get help, it's called anger management, not anger avoidance.

Marcus *feels* frustration sometimes, of course. He's not the emotionless saint his coworkers and friends make him out to be. But Marcus has self-control.

Someone with less self-control might have thrown the stapler straight into Marty's forehead and quit when Marty basically demanded that Marcus turn in his quarterly report a week early. "You aren't my boss, Marty!" an emotionally weaker employee might have screamed. "Duncan, tell Marty to leave me the hell alone from now on or I'll quit," he could have threatened. Mr. Duncan, the actual office manager, would have needed to listen because Marcus is a damn good employee.

Marcus doesn't threaten and make demands like that, though. That's exactly why Marcus would get what he wants if he did. When a person whines, threatens, and demands all the time, people stop listening to it. If, like Marcus, a man thoughtfully chooses his battles, then when he does ask for something, people listen. The squeaky wheel gets the oil, but the wheel that squeaks too much is the boy who cried wolf.

This is what Brynn doesn't understand.

Just two days ago, Sunday, she started crying over practically nothing, some small argument about whether the spinach goes in the right drawer or the left drawer. No big deal. She started crying about it, though. Then she put words in his mouth. He didn't say anything after she started crying. He didn't *do* anything. Yet she started saying he doesn't care about her. She says he "makes her feel" dumb. What is he? The magician of feelings?

If she wanted him to comfort her then she could have asked. Or at least if she did not fuss and cry, and make these wild accusations and cry, and yell and cry all the time, he would be more willing to comfort her or hug her when she does act like that. Brynn, the squeaky wheel, thinks that because she squeaks more, she feels more.

No, he feels plenty.

He gets frustrated. He gets his feelings hurt. But he expresses himself with words. Except he never gets a chance to explain himself because she's always too busy throwing a temper-tantrum every other day like a child.

He has hardly talked to her since Sunday, waiting for her to apologize. They used to make up quicker.

They would have a big fight where she got out of control. Then he would give her space. Then, when she calmed down, she would apologize because she hates the silent treatment. He always forgives her.

But he doesn't forgive her right away; he always tries to hold out for a while. If he holds out long enough, then she will really think about what happened and realize how screaming, crying, yelling, name-calling, and all of that nonsense just makes things so much worse.

When she gets mad she says such awful things, but then afterward, when she sees how much she hurt him because he is not talking to her, she finally apologizes.

Then it's too much of the opposite. Instead of saying whatever she can to hurt him, instead of all the screaming and name-calling, suddenly it's just her repeatedly promising it won't happen again. She's sorry, and yadda yadda... But then it does happen again. She refuses to think about it enough. He just has to give her time and space after these fights so she will think about it and see how childish she has acted, and start to change her behavior.

She would learn if he actually left her. If he actually refused to accept her apology for once. She would understand if he finally announced, "You always say it won't happen again. I've heard 'I'm sorry' too many times. It just doesn't mean anything to me anymore. I'm leaving you."

Well, he's said things like that, but if he actually left her she would remember those parting words. She would finally realize how badly she had messed things up. But it would be too late.

He never leaves her. He loves her too much. Maybe it's his fault that she behaves like that. He enables her. He encourages her with his constant forgiveness. It's simple, really: if he left her, she would learn. But he doesn't leave, so she doesn't learn.

He doesn't want to leave her. He loves her. If he just gives her enough of the silent treatment, then she can shape up and they can finally be happy together, without all the fighting.

Marcus is known not just for his patience but also for his intelligence. The two traits are, in essence, two aspects of the same trait: his thoughtfulness. So he realizes the silent treatment sounds a bit childish, but in comparison with her crazy angry screaming and swearing, it's really not. Most people would respond to her screaming with screaming. They would yell back... or worse.

Compared with how most people would respond to her childish, crazy behavior, Marcus deserves an award for handling her so well.

Maybe that reveals why they seem so meant-to-be. His patience matches her volatility. His thoughtfulness matches her impulsiveness.

Their relationship has unfolded like a roller coaster. Her craziness makes for a lot of big fights and bad times. Yet her wild impulsiveness also makes the good times so fun.

Without her, without amazing Brynn, he's basically just a bored, boring person.

Memories

Marcus so fondly remembers meeting her, the wildly wonderful, beautiful Brynn.

Early twenties... Friday night... Out with a few of his old friends from high school....

His friend Bobby had picked up Marcus to drive to bowling, of all things.

For the late Friday night crowd, this particular bowling alley replaced the normal lighting with dimmer, yet flashier, colored lights. The lighting matched the special Friday night 21-and-over policy.

While people were bowling, a waitress would eventually come around to take drink orders and then, as waitresses do, eventually bring the ordered drinks. In retrospect, it seemed that his own luck itself must have prevented that waitress from working with any kind of timeliness that night.

He met Brynn when he had briefly stepped away from his friends. Bobby needed another drink, so Marcus headed to the bar to grab another round for them both. Marcus is a good guy.

While leaning on the bar waiting for his drinks, his eyes caught those of the beautiful Brynn as she was walking by with her friend Tamara. Of course, at the time, Marcus didn't know their names. Nonetheless, Brynn smiled at him, waving gently as she and Tamara floated past. He waved back, but awkward and late somehow.

That really would have been it. But as things turned out, they had mutual friends. After Brynn and her friend Tamara left the bar, the two girls walked to lane eight to meet Bobby. Sure enough, when Marcus handed Bobby the gin and tonic, Bobby enthusiastically introduced Marcus to his coworker Tamara and his coworker Tamara's friend, Brynn.

Love at first sight? Not quite.

They talked and flirted a little, and they drank a lot.

Then they drank some more.

Through some drunken reasoning, revolving around pure logistics, it seemed logical to Brynn and Marcus that she would drive him home instead of Bobby.

Marcus gave Brynn a tour of his apartment. Then they had a lot of drunken sex.

For Marcus, the few weeks that followed were a blur. They aren't just a blur *now* from the wear and tear of time on memories. They *were* a blur *at the time*. A blur of going out with this exciting new girl, drinking, and having lots of sex.

Brynn burst into his life like a tornado of fun. The forceful winds of her presence tore away at the routine of life. Marcus smiles, remembering how he would speed home from work those first few months, so eager to meet up with Brynn, not wanting to miss a second.

He feasted on her beauty, on her playfulness, on her passion for life. This feast—this utter consumption—provided the energy to go through the motions of his daily routine.

His friends and family evolved into merely the audience to which to show off his new prize. The fact that he could snare a girl so incredible became his topmost unspoken brag.

Never, prior to her existence in his life, did he brush his teeth so thoroughly or shower so religiously. That little studio apartment on West 43rd Street had never been so clean.

He had never known such happiness.

She gave birth to him.

Gradually, the occasional evenings just staying in and watching movies together increased in frequency.

Eventually, staying in and watching movies turned into officially living together.

In between the initial occasional movies and the eventual living together, they toured Hal's Haunted Prison. Sometime later, they got married.

Many people declare their wedding day as their happiest day. Marcus loved his wedding and his bride. His favorite memory, however, has only one tangible artifact: a framed picture of Brynn standing in front of him with his arms wrapped warmly around her. A picture taken on a chilly day as their hair blew in the wind at the entrance of Hal's Haunted Prison.

It wasn't when he proposed to her. It wasn't where they met. Rather, it was one of those places, one of those memories, that is not marked by some cliché milestone or important anniversary. In fact, he could not tell you the date. It's one of those moments that just sticks with a man, perhaps precisely because it's otherwise so ordinary.

At one's own wedding or birthday party or some similar celebration, everyone expects the man of honor to have fun and be happy. So, when he has fun or is happy, it's really not remarkable or special. In fact, if someone says their wedding was "good"—*just good?*—it sounds *bad.* But Brynn made everything good. Truly good.

In that wonderful moment, touring the old prison, Marcus exploded with all the pride he had in his beautiful new girlfriend. Anyone can even see it for themselves in the picture, which hangs in a frame right in their living room. The picture shows, not the forced smiles, however realistically faked, of most pictures, but rather the true joy of their fortunate relationship.

Marcus never really felt alive until he met Brynn.

He loves her so much.

He will go home. She will come to him. They will make up, make love, and be happy.

More Traffic

Waiting in a line of cars caused by a lane merger, Marcus finally makes his way to the front of the bottleneck. One of the many impatient drivers slips in front of Marcus from the merging lane. Marcus presses on his breaks causing everyone in line, who merged early like the signs instructed, to once again step on their breaks.

Everyone could just go quickly if not for those few people trying to cheat. Don't they see that?

Marcus breathes in and out as he drives away. *Let it go.* He's known for his patience.

As his black Nissian approaches its driver's home on the right, Marcus has to pull gradually to the left. A neighbor's guest has parked a red Jeep in front of Marcus and Brynn's house. Maybe Marcus should park in front of the neighbors' house to see how they like it, but how would he know exactly which neighbors' house to target?

Like any other day, Marcus unlocks the deadbolt to his front door. *Like any other day.*

He could already hear the muffled voices, something indescribably ominous in their inflection.

Marcus opens the front door of the house, his house.

He catches only the last two words of a conversation. His gut drops, feeling empty and strained at the same time, as if his body parses the events before his mind. "Just go."

Brynn's voice. Not to Marcus. To the man walking through the kitchen towards the back door, the man clearly still adjusting his clothes.

A procession of nuclear bombs explode within Marcus's chest, pushing hot smoke through his veins, molten lava bubbling from his pores.

Marcus could chase the man through the kitchen. Marcus could go out the front, cut the man off before he reaches the red Jeep, the red Jeep whose driver is not a guest of one of the neighbors.

But what's the point? This strange man didn't betray Marcus. This strange man didn't even know Marcus to even be capable of jamming this cruel spear into Marcus's very soul. This strange man had done little wrong.

Marcus looks at Brynn. He sees her standing at the bottom of the stairs, between the kitchen and Marcus himself. In the living room between them hangs the picture from Hal's Haunted Prison.

"*Brynn...*" He whispers her name to her, not sure she can hear him from across the room. "Brynn, how... what have you done?"

She looks at him, and her words come out plainly, "We lost track of time."

As if all she did wrong was get caught!

She turns, heading up the stairs, past the picture.

"We better talk about this now, Brynn," Marcus calls after her. "If I leave, I'm never coming back."

No reply. She continues up the stairs.

He doesn't want to leave. He means it. If he leaves, he's not coming back. It's over for good. He doesn't want it to be over. He follows her up the stairs towards their bedroom.

Marcus walks into the bedroom and sees Brynn sprawled face-down on the bed. *Why?* As soon as he closes the door behind himself, she rises. A quick glance emits exasperation, before both her eyes and her body aim for the door.

"We need to talk about this now, Brynn. Now."

No reply. Her head turns sideways as she walks by him towards the bedroom door, her eyes again piercing at him through the air where his words still linger.

He notices Brynn's hand twisting aggressively on the door handle, barely noticing his own palm smack firmly over the crack between the door and the frame's edge. His voice louder now. "Has this happened before?!"

Maybe if it's the first time, he will be able to forgive her. She will need to work hard for his forgiveness, of course. And she would. She always comes crawling back. He can't just take her back, though. Of course not. If she thinks he's a pushover, she will just do it again. He needs to show her the unacceptability of her behavior. He needs her to be truly sorry. Then they can make up. Then they can be together and be happy.

"I don't owe you anything, Marcus. You owe me! I gave you all of me!" Her words slap him. She didn't even answer his question. She turns around towards the still-flickering candle on the end table. He pushes the back of her shoulder with his free hand, pushing her in the direction of the bed.

When he notices her run into the end table instead of the bed, his eyes, worried about a fire, trace the candle as it falls to the floor. She lets out a loud groan. He notices the blood mark on the wall where her forehead has dented the drywall.

He didn't mean to push her so hard, certainly not into the wall. He rushes to comfort her. To help her. But she screams loudly. What is she doing?! The neighbors will call the police. They will make an arrest first and ask questions later. They will take out a restraining order. He won't be able to see her. He places his left hand over her mouth, thumb down, pinky up, trying to muffle the noise. His left hand, his weak hand... *I'm not trying to hurt her.*

She squirms, screaming out of the corner of her mouth. Why is she doing this? She knows he wouldn't hurt her. She knows he is not a violent person. Does she actually want the police to come? Does she want him to be kicked out? What, so she can carry on with this other guy?

He wraps his free hand around the back of her head, holding her head in place, just so he can stop the noise with the hand on her mouth. She fights his grip, pretending as if he is actually trying to attack her like some kind of violent maniac. Why is she doing this to herself? His right hand loses its grip on the back of her neck and slides to the front because of her fighting. He tries to catch his grip by squeezing his right hand, his right hand that's on her neck, not choking her, just holding her. At the same time, her mouth becomes free.

She doesn't scream.

She spits on him!

He realizes her scowl, her grunts, her face... it all reveals anger and disgust more than fear.

He should be angry! She should feel fear and pain and loss. But he can't make her hurt as bad as she has hurt him. Nothing in the world compares to this kind of betrayal.

She will never hurt as bad as he hurts.

But she deserves to, he thinks, squeezing harder, both hands now on her neck. *This is justice.*

Part Three

The First Chair

The graying prosecutor sits comfortably in an uncomfortable chair—leaning back, legs extended to just-shy-of-straight, ankles crossed confidently. With his eyes on the full-audio security footage ready to be played on the screen, he enjoys a sip of his iced coffee. He imagines himself as a more cliché prosecutor, standing behind a two-way mirror sipping hot coffee from an old mug. He realizes life rarely resembles the movies. He realizes life is so much worse than the movies, much less dramatic but so much more anticlimactically awful. Just one mundane crap after another. On the other hand, his Large French Vanilla Iced Dunkin Donuts Coffee, pulled easily through the extra-wide plastic straw, tastes much better to him than hot coffee out of an old dirty TV mug.

Time has provided Joseph Bronson with more expertise than even his Harvard Law degree provided. Joseph would never speak ill of Harvard, though. Harvard gave him a top-notch education. Harvard also has a both excellent and vastly under-appreciated financial aid system, which he never needed himself but which he appreciates nonetheless.

However, experience always trumps education.

And time has made Joseph an expert on two things. And grayed his hair. But back to his expertise.

For exhibit one, consider Joseph's habit of enjoying various *Law and Order* episodes, consumed with moderate regularity in the two decades of time since he started his first internship. This pleasant habit made Joseph an expert in the many ways criminal justice *art* and criminal justice *reality* fail to mimic each other.

Despite—or perhaps *because of*—that failure, Joseph loves the shows and movies. He enjoys spotting the inconsistencies. He considers it similar to watching the movie adaption of a book after reading the book, or seeing the music video of a beloved song for the first time. Some people would hate it. He loves it.

Two decades in real life as a prosecutor has made Joseph an expert in a second area: the many follies that help destroy the lives of the unwilling actors who find themselves cast as the villains in this real-life version of Joseph's favorite TV show.

If you sit charged with a crime in front of a two-way mirror, you realize that someone like Prosecutor Joseph Bronson almost certainly watches from the other side—taking notes, preparing the snares. You recognize the whole setup as designed for the purpose of trapping you, not just chatting with you.

Yet these same people seem to ignore the security camera. Regulation requires the state's workers to inform the subject about the camera, at least to have any useful admissibility. Consciously these targets know it's there. You can even see the camera in the room. But the targets always seem more relaxed than with a mirror or an actual audience. People react to eyeballs, not cameras. They react to clichés and stereotypes, not the dangerous reality in front of their faces.

Joseph doubts the choice to use cameras instead of mirrors stems from some clever design to get more arrests and convictions. Rather, many of the ways people help drag themselves to the slaughter just happen naturally. You don't really need some chess Grandmaster's plan to snag a deer in the headlights—a person under investigation who has no lawyer, to drop the metaphor.

Of course, the prosecutors and the police still eagerly play chess against these people—well, kids mostly.

The oldest trick in the book? Well, these kids do not have a lawyer to actually act as their real friend, to act as their real advisory, so the police play the part. And the show goes on.

"I want to help you. You can trust me. Just sign this paper... Oh, it's just everything you said, but I typed it for you."

"Sure, you have 'the right' to remain silent. But your vehicle registration expired. I was going to let that go with a warning..."

"Don't you want to go home today? I just need you to cooperate. Who cares if you have a little marijuana in the car? I just want to make sure there are no guns, nothing dangerous. So just tell me if you have a little marijuana. Just be honest with me, and we can all go home."

"You help me, and I'll help you."

"You could bail your son out tonight, ma'am. But court's in the morning, and so far he's only been charged with a misdemeanor. An overnight in the holding cell will teach him a lesson so he doesn't get it worse next time. Leave him here; it'll be good for him."

These poor people could achieve near *prosecutorial invulnerability* by simply refusing to talk at all until they get a lawyer. Half of them would not even get arrested in the first place. For those that had the chains slapped on, a public defender would eventually come. Simply not talking would give these people ninety percent of what a lawyer does: keep the *burden of proof* where basic principle says it goes.

But public defenders show up quite a bit later than on the drop of a hat. Your phone never rings with urgent calls from the public defender's office urging you to remain silent. Only rich people seem comfortable with the seemingly rude blow-off, "Talk to my lawyer."

Joseph turns to face the sound. The door creaks as it opens, rudely interrupting Joseph's daily internal diatribe. Some blue-uniformed workhorse stands there, staring wide-eyed at Joseph. *I forget his name.* "Oh, sorry, Sir, I didn't know you were still in here."

"It's fine."

"I'll let you get back to it. Oh, while I have you, we're getting some lunch from Elmer's Seaside in a bit. Can I grab you something, Mr. Bronson?

"Hm, yeah, the Lobster Plate. Make sure it's the large. Here you can put it on my AmEx—the whole thing. Yours too. It's nothing."

Joseph holds the card out. The man stares for a moment doing the calculation. He can't reach the card from the door. He's going to have to walk over. *I'm not getting up.*

The uniform grabs the card and finally leaves. Joseph sighs, leans back again, and considers pressing play. *Talk to my lawyer...*

It's all mostly irrelevant anyway. Convictions rarely matter.

Who goes to jail and who goes home has almost nothing to do with the accuracy of the accusations of guilt.

Who goes to jail depends most of all on who has bail money. If you have bail money, you go home. If you cannot afford bail, any cop on a whim can throw you in jail for months if not years without a conviction. Even that nice boy grabbing the lobster—he could arrest any random person on trumped up charges and ruin that person's life, assuming the victim cannot afford bail and a lawyer.

Even when a conviction eventually comes, the sentence often comes out as time-served, meaning fighting your charges in court frequently leads to more jail time than taking a plea deal. Even an innocent person generally finds himself much better off taking the plea deal.

Plenty of innocent people fight their charges, for whatever foolish reason, and still get convicted and sentenced to prison. The invention of DNA tests revealed the incredible ease with which the court system delivers false convictions. Depending on the study one chooses to use, 55,000 to 120,000 human beings in prison in the United States right now are innocent.

In fact, a National Institute of Justice study demonstrated that conducting DNA testing during investigations excluded targets in more than 25 percent of cases. But DNA cannot be used in the vast majority of cases. *Ugh.* Joseph shakes his head to himself. This is his life. *Nobody else cares. It all just bores them.*

If not by guilt or the heinousness of the offense, then what determines which victims of the legal system go to prison?

Well, what are the odds some rich kid's father doesn't play golf with the judge, and isn't a doctor who treats the police chief, and isn't a contributor to that judge's election campaign, and isn't anything to that judge or that chief?

Guilty, rich, white people usually don't go to jail. And innocent, poor, black kids very often do. And sometimes even well-to-do, innocent, white people go to jail. Sometimes even innocent, pretty, wealthy women get tossed in the slammer. It's not completely black and white. It's a gamble. The odds are much worse for some than others, but it's a gamble nonetheless—a gamble with odds bearing almost no relation to actual guilt.

Joseph could easily help any of these young boys. He wouldn't need to whip out his big, strong lawyer expertise to do it. For the ones who cross his path, he could simply let them go. Most of them have only minor charges. Even the big charges—the felonies—are usually for nonviolent crimes.

Just last week, Joseph had a scheduling hearing for some kid who got caught with the last quarter inch of a joint in a parked car across the street from Newbury High School—a felony. Kid is still in jail right now; will be for a long time. If he doesn't take a plea, the jury won't even get selected for a few more months.

Nobody in the courthouse even gives a second thought to the stream of young boys flowing through. How much does a cashier think about any one of the hundreds of customers she cashes out in a single shift?

Thus we find the answer to the question: 'Why *not* help any of them?'

A question answered with a question: 'Why *help* any of them?'

Or more accurately: 'Why help any *one* of them?'

Joseph is a good guy. He turned in his homework during Miss Fletcher's third grade class. He didn't decapitate the Hanson's dog like that weirdo Bill. Bill who has now already worked his way to vice executive of a top investment firm with nothing seeming to slow the momentum of his luxurious career.

Why this, why that...

Why wouldn't good old Joe call out sick from work, pack a few cases of Powerbars into a suitcase, buy a plane ticket to Ethiopia, and go feed a kid who will literally starve to death if Joseph does not do it? Why not save one innocent child's life? Well, Joseph could save a kid's life, but Joseph cannot afford twenty thousand cases of Powerbars. He can't take twenty thousand days off from work. He can't buy twenty thousand plane tickets.

Twenty thousand children starve to death every day.

Some single kid starving to death in the third-world is simply typical.

If Joseph tells the judge one day to let some kid off with a slap on the wrist for a crime that usually leads to significant jail time, the judge would not bat an eye. That works once, not twenty thousand times. Using a teaspoon to try to scoop water off the Titanic would waste less time and effort.

And there are not merely twenty thousand people rotting in jails and prisons in the United States today. There are over two million.

One poor teenager without a Harvard Law degree getting railroaded? Just a drop of water in the fast river constantly flowing through the justice department.

Typical.

What's not typical is what Joseph sees on this screen today.

A white man. *Not typical.*

Looks middle-class enough to afford a lawyer if he needs one. *Not typical.*

Charged with a violent crime. *Not typical.*

Accused of murdering his wife. *Not- Well, as far as murders go, that one has some typicality to it.*

With his eyes off the screen for a moment, Joseph smiles, not because of anything on the screen and not because he takes joy in the suspect's precarious situation, but rather because he still has more than half of his Large French Vanilla Iced Dunkin Donuts Coffee.

Joseph sips eagerly, wondering if it is actually an act this time; you know, the buddy-buddy act put on by the slightly-chubby, slightly-tall detective Joseph knew as Will Barnes.

Home

"So you got that case?" Marie asks. "The one all over the news? Cool! Big case."

Joseph grins at his wife, sliding off his designer suit jacket. "When the state needs a great prosecutor for a big case, of course they come to me. Why do you even seem surprised?"

"Next time, instead of a big case they might give you *The Modesty Award*."

"If only they had one, I'd win every time."

"Dammit!" Dropping the half-gallon water-filtering jug she just finished refilling with liquid from the kitchen sink, Marie rescues at least half the water by quickly retrieving the jug from the floor. Unfortunately, several glasses worth of water are splattered all over the floor and cabinets like wet flames from a grenade. "How about you strangle me to death, Joseph. You know, to get in your client's head."

Joseph laughs earnestly, while futilely attempting to resist the urge to correct his wife. "He isn't my client, Marie. He's the defendant. I'm the Wile E. to his Road Runner. I mean, if the coyote caught the bird, that is."

"Right. Anyway, have fun upstairs with all those interesting-looking papers."

Joseph appreciates the short conversation with Marie. They hardly get any time together anymore.

They could make time, but he has his job. Besides, she somehow already manages to rock out at the PTA in addition to taking care of their two daughters. She basically maintains their large house completely on her own.

She stays up late nights reading; he wakes up early mornings for work. He likes dropping by Juice's Bar on his way home from work; she likes to get lunch at Panera Bread. He occasionally squeezes in an episode of *Law and Order* which she refuses to watch; she occasionally splurges with some shopping at the mall where he refuses to go. Sometimes he brings his work home in the evenings; sometimes she makes it out for coffee with her friend Sarah or to the rotating location of the official Mom's Book Club.

He still likes his wife, though. They get along well, always have. The passion did die, not just die but totally get obliterated.

He cannot imagine strangling her, however. Not only would he never strangle anyone, but also he does not have anything close to that kind of anger towards her. He still loves her, as the mother of his kids, as the co-parent in this business of maintaining a house and raising children.

The wear of a romance-less relationship can easily fertilize resentment, the seedling of that kind of anger. Joseph's a smart guy; he knows that. Without the children, maybe his path could have looked a lot more like Marcus Malley's path.

Luckily then for Joseph, kids teach their parents a new romance-less love, more powerful perhaps than the passionate exploding emotions of young lovers. He still loves his wife just as he loves his kids, a special brotherly love lacking even the rivalry of siblings. He gets along with her even better than he gets along with the kids. Marie is a lot more reasonable than the girls, especially the hormonal one.

Of course, he misses the passionate lovemaking and the drunken feeling he could get just from spending time with her. He misses blabbering together about whatever dumb thoughts they each had until 2am, somehow still at that late hour feeling the excitement one might expect from skydiving.

He misses it not in an angry way. He misses it not in a depressed way.

He misses it as an elderly man misses his childhood dog—more like a pleasant nostalgia with just a sprinkle of longing.

He misses the passion he used to have for his job too. In fact, his job really killed the romance of his marriage, more than the kids. That's probably true for most marriages, though, probably even Marcus Malley's fateful marriage.

See, it's not that Joseph's incredible passion for his job overpowered the strength of his passion for Marie. It's not that he lost his passion for his wife faster than he lost it for his job.

It's that you can stop going on dates each weekend, but you can't stop getting up for work five days a week. You forget birthdays and anniversaries faster than you forget deadlines and court dates, regardless of how dispassionately remembered.

If anything, he lost his passion for his job *faster* than he lost it for his wife. He would have *chosen* to keep his passion with Marie over his passion for his job.

He would strangle his job if he could.

He would strangle the whole damn criminal court system. He would strangle the prisons and strangle the police stations. He would strangle each of the millions of words of law. Words! Millions upon millions of them! So many words that no person could read them all in a lifetime.

"What would we do with the criminals?!" the people would cry.

The imaginary naysayers' question makes no sense. With so many laws, everyone is a criminal.

If you smoke marijuana, you are a criminal. If you do not follow all four million words of the United States Tax Code—that's just the tax code!—you're a criminal. If you speed on the highway, well then you get to wear the *dangerous* criminal hat, bordering on graduating to *violent* criminal.

Signing in to your neighbor's unsecured WiFi? Illegal. *What if your phone does it automatically?* Still illegal.

Letting your kids start a lemonade stand? Illegal. *What if you give all the proceeds to charity?* Still illegal.

Riding in the passenger seat of your friend's car without a seat-belt? Illegal. *What if the cop who pulled you over on the highway was riding on a motorcycle?* Still illegal.

Marital rape? Well, that was legal in some US states until 1993, a time when Joseph was already working in the system, but now that's illegal too. The illegality of that one Joseph supports, though.

Joseph likes seeing rape starting to almost hold as severe a penalty as marijuana possession.

Speaking of marijuana, Missouri sentenced Jeff Mizanskey to life in prison for marijuana. Speaking of incarceration, South Carolina jailed Kayla Michelle Finley for failing to return a VHS she rented from Dalton Videos, out-of-business by the time Miss Finley was jailed. California police arrested Cindy Hahn for not wearing a seat-belt. Florida repeatedly jailed the charitable 90-year-old Arnold Abbott for feeding the homeless. True stories. All of them.

It was harder to get someone burned at the stake for witchcraft centuries ago than it is to find an excuse nowadays to send some mouthy city kid—or some generous elderly man—to the pound.

Nobody cares. Joseph can't say these silent words aloud, at least not without a few drinks at Juice's Bar. He would bore people, lose friends, and suck as a prosecutor. Nobody wants an exposé. He'd lose his third car, and that's what people want. He sits down alone in his large upstairs home office, scanning the rich mahogany desk.

True stories... By making everyone a criminal, those with discretion get a blank check.

Police get a book of blank checks. DCF workers get a book of blank checks. Judges get a book of blank checks. Parole officers. Prison guards. And, of course, prosecutors.

Almost a decade of Harvard wasn't easy. But this job is. It's like shooting fish in a barrel.

2.2 million people do not end up in prison when you shoot at a moving target.

A person can't strangle prisons and courts, though. And Joseph wouldn't strangle actual people. *Nobody deserves to die.*

That's why that ignorant fool, Young Joey, applied to Harvard Law. Joey would protect us from stranglers. Joey would help the criminal justice system put stranglers into prison. Prisons protect us from violent people. Courts convict those proven guilty, proven beyond a reasonable doubt. Police carefully investigate crimes, making discretionary arrests based on the evidence and the heinousness of the crime. And Young Joey would grow old eating a home-cooked meal *every single night* on the nice china *every single night* while sitting together with his wife *every single night* before making sweet passionate love to her *every single night for over half of a century*. The system works, and true passion lasts forever.

Footage

With a fresh Large French Vanilla Iced Dunkin Donuts Coffee, Joseph replays the footage he watched yesterday of Detective Barnes playing buddy-buddy in the interrogation room.

The case seems open and shut regarding a conviction on the facts, but a lot of very guilty people go Scot-free on some *i* that didn't get dotted or some *t* that didn't get crossed.

More than that, though, the real trial, the real challenge, will come after conviction. This is a capital case. The real case is the sentencing.

Joseph wants to get a feel for this defendant. Joseph wants to understand him. Joseph indeed *needs* to understand the man, as a matter of Joseph's career, but also a part of Joseph simply *wants* to understand the man. So Joseph studies the screen carefully.

"What's your game here, Marcus? Is this some kind of passive aggressive trick? Are you trying to play criminal mastermind? Do you think if you don't defend yourself people will think you feel guilty or something? You think, then, they won't want you dead?"

After leaving about zero seconds for his rhetorical questions to sink in, the tall chubby Detective known as Barnes continued, "You couldn't be more off, Marcus. They want your blood. You're not a person to all those people out there. You're just a character, a monster of a character, in a play—a play being put on in the media. Well, they got that part right. What you did is monstrous. And you'll never change what they think of you. Especially not with silly games. Even if you got the best attorney in the world and got acquitted, they would still want your blood. You would probably need security for life. Anything else they get besides your blood will just upset them more—make them more bloodthirsty. If there was any chance of leniency they would have offered you a plea. They never even considered letting you keep your life as so much as a bargaining chip. Not even considered."

Taking a few deep breaths while the redness in his face subsided, Detective Barnes patted his suit-jacket down over his slight potbelly. Barnes seemed like he actually wanted to help the young man—give some good advice. Some men spend their whole lives playing Daddy.

"You don't use the PD in a capital case, Marcus; it's stupid. You're being ridiculously unreasonable. Ri-dic-u-lous."

"I wouldn't think my demographic-"

"Your demographic?" interrupted Barnes, a man whose frequent unrequited curiosity seemed symptomatic of aggressive self-importance.

"Inmates facing death row." A moment of actual silence finally emerged before Marcus continued, "I wouldn't think my demographic was known for our reasonableness."

Ha.

Joseph grins.

See, this is why I hate capital punishment. This guy seems kind of cool, aside from the whole spouse-slaughtering thing of course. I will really dislike trying to kill him.

Office

Months after first receiving the Marcus Malley case, Joseph leans forward over his office desk, scanning through various paperwork prepared by the interns and the many other human cogs of the multibillion-dollar bustling bureaucracy of real life *Law and Order*. Joseph both rushes through the task and takes many breaks to stare at the ceiling, leaning back in his solid 50lb leather chair.

Joseph still recalls a time before two decades of a job well done earned him the esteemed privilege of shirking grunt work—no easy task in a system that makes itself seem overworked and underfunded by diverting most of its resources to caging nonviolent or innocent people.

In his days as an intern, Joseph excitedly spent hours jumping through the hoops of all sorts of legal code to properly prepare documents. Like the other interns and newbies, he felt honored when selected by one of the 'real live trial lawyers' as the go-to person to delegate a task.

Nowadays, after dumping hours of labor on some borderline nameless workhorse, he despises even the tedious task of quickly reviewing their work.

The interns and newbies do a great job. Even the unpaid interns love it. They want to earn their position, their heroic position standing powerfully and proudly between society and violent maniacs.

The real mystery is why the newbies think, and by extension why Joseph used to think, that achieving the incredible honor of standing between those two things would have anything to do with handling the bureaucracy of putting nonviolent black kids in prison.

Even if one of these interns sees some value in imprisoning these poor kids by the millions, for such an intern a disappointment awaits, the disappointment of learning how little their paperwork has to do with it.

Unless the defense has some expensive attorney who would bother going through all these piles of crap, or making *his* interns do it, then it matters more what the judge ate for lunch than how hard the interns and clerks work.

Multiple studies have shown parole approvals decline as the day wears on, until lunch of course. Parole judges grant parole three times as often right after lunch. A similar pattern surely happens with the sentencing of impoverished people for prostitution, marijuana, or unpaid tickets.

Prison isn't for violent people put away thanks to the hard work of bureaucrats; it's for nonviolent people who are unlucky.

"What are you daydreaming about, boss?" asks one of the more outgoing newbies.

If only you knew, Joseph thinks. "Nothing much," Joseph says. "I think I'll call it a day and head over to Juice's Bar. You guys can feel free to come by for a round on me when you're done with the Charleston file."

After Some Months

As the months had passed, the Marcus Malley case had consumed more and more of Joseph's thoughts, not just because of the case itself but also because of the way the local media grasped onto the story in the way a cute pitbull tears at a juicy cut of tenderloin.

The court of public opinion already delivered a ferocious verdict of guilt, guilt not just of fact but of character in the deepest sense. No amount of harm inflicted on Mr. Malley would satisfy their eager, awaiting blood-lust. They wordlessly delivered the orders to Joseph loud and clear: *pull the trigger.*

Indeed, the court, the bloated books of law, the hopefully hungry judge, those were all parts of the gun in Joseph's hand, pointed straight at Marcus Malley. Joseph is neither the captain nor the weapon.

If Joseph possessed the omnipotence of gods and kings, he would ban the death penalty and all intentional homicide. *Nobody deserves to die.*

But he has a job to do, and he feels confident in winning both the conviction and the sentencing.

Joseph knows he will—*he must*—pull the trigger. Joseph knows he will—*he must*—kill Mr. Marcus Malley.

After Some More Months

"Try to get your homework done before you fool around on the computer," the aging mother calls after her daughters as the girls skip upstairs.

The older one looks back, smirking. "We use the computers to do our homework, Mom."

"I know; I know. Just do something productive on it before you look at pictures of cats, okay?"

The girls say a few things to each other that Mom can't hear. They giggle and disappear upstairs.

Joseph glances from his spot at the dinner table, cleared for a while of the remains of dinner. His notebooks lie on the table in front of him, but most of the work now occurs in his head.

The supportive woman speaks to him gently, "The case must be over soon?"

"I'm working on my closing statements now."

Joseph smiles to her with a sense of camaraderie. Have they really talked so little since he first got this case all those months ago?

Joseph loves his wife. He loves her for her continued loyalty through the years. He loves her for wholeheartedly mothering their two beautiful daughters. He loves her, perhaps most of all, because of the passion they once shared.

Young people intoxicated by new romance dream of sharing a wondrous future together consisting of some fanciful montage of tingly hand-holding, sweet forehead kisses, and ever more lustful lovemaking.

The curse of life, not just love life but all life, reveals itself in the humdrum of the daily, the antithesis of the montage.

The best always lasts for a mere fleeting moment, an infinitesimally small point in the strange dimension of time.

This pattern manifests all around.

A new car plummets in value as soon as the excited new owner peels off the lot. After long hours building a dream home, the home begins to deteriorate the moment construction ends. The beautiful lasts but a moment; the rubble lasts an eternity.

All pleasures, both the great and the routine, taste of the bittersweet reminder of the perfection away from which they inherently flow.

"What are you thinking about?" she asks.

If only you knew, Joseph thinks. "I love you," he says.

Bar

The big black man saunters towards Joseph, eyes locked on Joseph's. The big man's loud words come out like a quick stream of barks.

Then he hands his buddy Joseph a new Manhattan. "That's number two, Joey Boy," he barks. "I'll keep track, and if you have too many I'll make you stay here until I close up four hours from now."

Juice always jokes about making Joseph stay until close. Apparently, that would include Joseph doing large amounts of what Juice calls side-work.

"Aww, Joey, don't tell me you're all melancholy today? You're always so melancholy when you come in here before the end of a big case."

"Damn, Juice, I make one joke about 'college words' and it's 'melancholy' this and 'melancholy' that."

"Well, I know I'm just a stodgy bartender... but we did go to law school together."

"You dropped out!"

"I won the lottery!"

"Your father died!" Joseph feigns disgust in good humor. He knows Juice had worshiped, uh, Juice Senior. Juice's cold joke merely halfheartedly covered up a terrible old wound that continues to remain a painful scar.

"Yes, but... my father had a lot of money saved up. Money he refused to share with me while still breathing. To teach me how to take care of myself. This is why I had to bartend to barely survive in college. *Harvard*." Juice left the words lingering in the musty bar air for a moment. "I couldn't have dropped out and bought this here fancy bar with my daddy's money had I not learned both the skill and the work ethic to go along with it."

Juice pretends he left law school just because his inheritance had given him enough to open his own business. Joseph knows the emotional crippling of Juice's father's unexpected heart attack had contributed more to his dropping out than just having the financial option.

"Anyway, don't try to turn this on me," Juice barks. Juice barked almost everything, usually from halfway across the bar. Sometimes instead of barking he would lean in real close to practically whisper. "Stop melancholy-ing up the place."

"You know the drill, Juice. I like to come see my staunch Republican friend to get pumped up before I get people convicted."

"It's true that I am a strong, handsome, Bible-thumping, flag-waving, Christian conservative man. And a small-business-owner, I might add. A handsome small-business owner. But I thought this case would be right up your cynical alley, Joey Boy," the bartender jeers. "A middle-class white guy actually getting strung up. Isn't that what you dream about at night? Isn't that why poor Marie has to wash the bedsheets so often?"

Both men turn when another man sitting about four seats down the bar calls out, "I thought you said you were a prosecutor; which side are you on?!" The man yells like a protester but snorts playfully.

"You know the story," Juice quickly answers. Joseph lifts the whiskey to his mouth, seeing as he cannot answer for himself. "Because if some thug whose skin happens to be dark commits a crime and gets caught, *it's society's fault.*"

"You realize that saying what I believe with a sarcastic tone doesn't actually provide any evidence against it, right?"

"Don't lawyer me, Joey, or I'll call your tab."

"I don't have a tab," Joseph counters fast, his eyebrows narrowed towards a point about three inches above an inquisitive grin.

"You will when I bill you for all those free shots and over-pours over the past twenty years."

"Hah, now you're the lawyer."

"Well, I'll be a real one, not a whiny little baby who complains about putting criminals behind bars."

Joseph stands up, writes a zero in the tip line like always, and signs the little piece of paper. He slides his card in his wallet, slides out two of many twenty dollar bills, and tosses the pair next to the card receipt. "Has it really been twenty years?" Joseph quickly tosses the tumbler back, holding the glass up high for a moment to let the whole last delicious sip drain, the rhetoric of his question filling the silence. "I need to find a new bar."

"And what? Give your business to some nice white man or some 'Big Mean Corporation' instead of patronizing me? I'd love to see it from you, Joey! Here's to your farewell." Juice refills both the used tumbler and a new one, each with an ounce of crisp, brown whiskey. Juice half-hardheartedly pushes the used tumbler two inches in Joseph's direction. Both men throw back their shot. "See you in two days, Joey! Good luck."

Reality

A long time ago, Juice had once asked Joseph a stunning question. "You know, Joey, doing my job I hear a lot of people complaining about their jobs. You could say I make a living off the many people who hate their jobs. If the drinks didn't cheer up these poor souls, it would be a sad sight to see. But a prosecutor with this much disdain for the system, that I just can't believe. Man, it's unreal! If I didn't know you, I would never believe you exist. You chose to be a prosecutor. You're not a slave, my friend. I don't understand it. Why don't you just quit?"

Joseph had meant to bring up that topic again with Juice.

Joseph would have asked Juice, *can you understand a man who has so much disdain for his wife that he strangles her to death?*

Court

Tired from long hours at a long trial, the jury nonetheless feels the powerful influx of energy pouring inside of them from the charismatic veteran prosecutor. The silently electrified jurors listen carefully as Prosecutor Joseph Bronson continues his closing statements.

"This man, Marcus Malley, brutally murdered this beautiful woman in the prime of her life.

"The defense might have you believe he had a moment of rage. 'It could happen to anyone. He's not evil.'

"I don't know about you, but I've been angry before. Very angry.

"I don't kill people, though. I don't murder people. I don't wrap my hand around your neck because I am mad at you.

"That's the rub of it, though; isn't it?

"This man didn't suddenly turn his gun on his wife in a moment of anger during an outing at the shooting range. He didn't shoot her at all.

"He struggled to knock her down. He wrapped his hands around her neck. One single hand at a time.

"That's not some wild claim. That's what he said!

"In his own confession of his brutal attack on his wife... he didn't say he grabbed her in a sudden rage.

"He took his time, one single hand at a time, like a man with a plan. He squeezed and squeezed and squeezed.

"He made a decision, a thought-out decision, to end Brynn Malley's life. He could have changed that decision anytime as he slowly choked every bit of life from her. All it would have taken is one moment—one moment—of indecision. One breath. Literally,

one breath. One breath of consideration from him and one life-saving breath of oxygen for this beautiful woman, Brynn Malley.

"It takes more than five minutes to kill someone by strangulation. He continued second after second, minute after minute, squeezing the neck of her unconscious body with his bare hands. Second after second. Minute after minute. Watching her die. Wanting her to die. Choosing for her to die.

"Actions must have consequences. The punishment must fit the crime. We don't have the death penalty for joy. This isn't good. This isn't fun. This isn't for pleasure. This is justice."

Part Four

The Last Chair

Knowing its destination, Marcus watches the fateful poison—sodium thiopental—gradually escape the container.

Moments pass.

I thought I would be dead by now.

Marcus realizes everyone has a last thought, whether they know it or not. The most dramatic and least remembered thought of each of their lives...

Marcus gazes at the empty container. More moments pass.

Marcus wishes he could choose his last thought.

This is justice.

He wants that to be it. He wants that to be his last thought.

But it isn't.

His last thought is more of a fantasy—a memory. He sees himself—remembers himself—holding Brynn's hand by a fake tree in the mall all those years ago. Staring at her. Smiling. She smiled back, so brightly... so sweetly. Oh, that connection... that connection you feel so thoroughly. The emotional equivalent of staring into the sun. *What a beautiful love.*

The End

Discussion questions on next page.

Discussion Questions

These questions are posted at OnlineBookClub.org. Go there to view other people's answers and share your own answers.

Question 1 ~ Brynn Malley vs. Prosecutor Joseph Bronson

In the first part, Brynn seems to suggest people would think poorly of her if she told them she was allegedly being emotionally abused. She seems to believe that people *"want small talk, not to play mad libs or listen to you whine about your life"*. Later, in the part with Prosecutor Joseph Bronson, on several occasions Joseph laments that *"nobody cares,"* particularly in parts of the story while he rants about the criminal justice system. What similarities and differences do you see between these two characters, their complaints, and how they deal with what they believe makes them unhappy?

Question 2 ~ Children

Brynn briefly makes a reference to the idea of having children. What did you make of that reference? Do you think Brynn wanted children and if so do you think she communicated those desires to Marcus? If she wanted children, why didn't it come up more in the story? Prosecutor Joseph Bronson seems to suggest that his marriage may have turned out like Marcus Malley's marriage if Joseph and his wife hadn't had children. Do you think that's true?

Question 3 ~ The Squeaky Wheel

In Part 2, Marcus complains, *"Brynn, the squeaky wheel, thinks that because she squeaks more, she feels more."* Ignoring for a moment the events that come after that, who do you think was the victim in their relationship? Who do you think was more to blame for the martial problems they were having?

Question 4 ~ See How They Like It

When Marcus gets home in Part 2, he sees a red jeep that he believes is one of the neighbor's and considers parking in front of the neighbor's house to *"see how they like it"*. Do you think this is significant? How does it relate to Marcus and to the events in the story?

Question 5 ~ Good Guys vs. Bad Guys

In Part 3, Prosecutor Joseph Bronson spends a lot of time complaining about the criminal justice system, the same system for which he works and which he helps make possible. He even possibly seems to describe the criminals as the victims. Do you think he makes a fair representation by doing that? Do you think Joseph's view is too one-sided? If so, how does it relate to Brynn's and Marcus's different views of their relationship? Who's the victim in these different situations? Who are the good guys, and who are the bad guys?

Question 6 ~ Utter Consumption

Part 2, which follows Marcus Malley, describes at one point the story of Marcus meeting Brynn. This description includes the following paragraphs:

Brynn burst into his life like a tornado of fun. The forceful winds of her presence tore away at the routine of life. Marcus smiles, remembering how he would speed home from work those first few months, so eager to meet up with Brynn, not wanting to miss a second.

He feasted on her beauty, on her playfulness, on her passion for life. This feast—this utter consumption—provided the energy to go through the motions of his daily routine.

His friends and family evolved into merely the audience to which to show off his new prize. The fact that he could snare a girl so incredible became his topmost unspoken brag.

Never, prior to her existence in his life, did he brush his teeth so thoroughly or shower so religiously. That little studio apartment on West 43rd Street had never been so clean.

He had never known such happiness.

She gave birth to him.

Can you relate to this feeling? How does it jive with the ultimate fate of their relationship and marriage? How does it compare to Prosecutor Joseph Bronson's relationship with his wife?

Question 7 ~ Marcus Malley vs. Joseph Bronson

Part 2 starts with a wordy monologue of Marcus complaining about Brynn. In Part 3, Prosecutor Joseph Bronson complains a lot about the criminal justice system. What are the other similarities and differences between these two characters? What do you imagine are the similarities and differences in how they each feel about their respective marriages and jobs?

Question 8 ~ Real Love

Both Marcus Malley and Prosecutor Joseph Bronson are described as loving their respective wives. Do you think each of them really loved their wives? Do you think Brynn Malley loved Marcus? Do you think Marie Bronson loved her husband? Do you think Joseph and Marie loved their children? Do you think Joseph Bronson loved the criminal *"boys"* in the *"fast river constantly flowing through the justice department"*? Do you think Joseph loved the people he helped get sentenced to death by capital punishment? Why or why not?

Question 9 ~ Killing

Prosecutor Joseph Bronson is repeatedly described as trying to "kill" Marcus Malley. However, he does this so-called "killing" by using his veteran skills as a prosecutor to get Marcus convicted and legally sentenced to death. How does Joseph "killing" Marcus compare and contrast to a husband killing his spouse? Is one just and the other not? Why or why not?

Question 10 ~ To Whom Do You Relate?

Brynn seems to blame her misery on Marcus emotionally abusing her. Marcus plainly describes being cheated on as hurting him more than she could ever hurt. Even before finding out about the cheating, Marcus seems to blame Brynn for his misery. Prosecutor Joseph Bronson seems to feel betrayed by his job and presumably blames his misery on that. Can you relate to any or all of these characters? Have you ever been emotionally abused? Have you ever been cheated on? Have you ever had a job you hate? Which do you think is worse? If you were in any of these situations before, how bad was it?

Question 11 ~ Miserable Situations

When someone is in a miserable situation—such as being in a broken marriage, being emotionally abused, being cheated on, or being in a job one hates—how much responsibility should that person take for their own problems? How do you feel about the ways the characters in *Justice* dealt with their respective situations?

Question 12 ~ Just Quit

Brynn could have both either chosen to work on her marriage or divorce her husband instead of cheating on him. Equally, Marcus could have either chosen to work on his marriage or divorce his wife instead of doing what he did to her. Near the end of the book, Juice asks Joseph *"why don't you just quit?"* Why do you think Joseph doesn't quit? Do you think Joseph has a lot in common with Brynn and/or Marcus? Is it possible that's what makes Joseph such a good prosecutor?

Question 13 ~ The Rubble Lasts an Eternity

In Part 3, Joseph explains that "the beautiful lasts but a moment; the rubble lasts an eternity." Do you think this is true? Do you think it tells more about reality or about Joseph's own outlook? How do you think Marcus would feel about this outlook at the beginning of the book? What about near the end? How do you think Brynn would feel about this outlook at the beginning of the book?

Question 14 ~ Juice

What did you make of the character Juice? Do you think he is a likable character? How does the interaction between Juice and Joseph affect the story, if at all? Do you think it was well-placed?

Juice mocks Joseph for allegedly blaming society instead of criminals. In part, Juice calls his friend Joseph *"a whiny little baby who complains about putting criminals behind bars"*. Do you think this is a fair description?

Question 15 ~ Why Only Juice

Why do you think Joseph seems to admit his intense criticisms of the criminal justice system only to Juice? Do you think he also talks to Juice—and only Juice—about how he feels about his marriage and how he feels in general? Do you think Joseph would be better or worse if he honestly described his feelings to more people?

Question 16 ~ Lonely

Brynn Malley had a lot of intimate interactions with numerous 'friends'; do you think she still felt lonely? Do you think Marcus Malley felt lonely? Do you think Joseph felt lonely? What about Joseph's wife? What about Juice? Do you think some of them felt lonely at some points in the story but not at other points in the story? How do you think these feelings relate to the first sentence of the book in the preface: *"Sympathy shines the only light in the dark impassable tunnels constructed between all of us."*

www.ingramcontent.com/pod-product-compliance
Lightning Source LLC
Chambersburg PA
CBHW020930310726
48980CB00007B/700/J

9780692636992